TŪĪ
Does it Tough

Written and Illustrated by Paul Prosée

Deep in the forest, Tūī flutters around.
His tuft of white feathers, nowhere to be found.
Darting this way and that, up high and down low.
Hours of searching, with nothing to show.

"Where are they?" cried Tūī, deep in despair.
"I've lost them. I've lost them. And I just don't know where.
What should I... what should I... what should I do?
There's nothing right there where my neck feathers grew."

Tūī stopped for a moment, for a breath and a think.
A thought popped in his head, as quick as a wink.
The thought that he had, that thought did suggest
to go and see Ruru, for he would know best.

"He's so wise," thought Tūī, "much wiser than most.
Yet so very humble, he's not one to boast.
He'll surely give me, a hint or a clue
about somewhere to start, or just what to do."

3

"M-o-r-e-p-o-r-k, m-o-r-e-p-o-r-k," was the sound Tūī followed,
to find Ruru perched, in a pūriri tree hollow.
"Who are you?" hooted Ruru, "I'm a little befuddled.
Why don't I know you? Is my memory so muddled?"

"It's me!" replied Tūī. "You know me real well."
"My mistake," tooted Ruru. "I just could not tell.
Without your white tuft, you don't ring any bells."

Tūī took a deep breath, and let out a sigh.
"I really don't know, how I will get by.
I'm not who I am, it's tough, can't you see?
Without my white tuft, I just can't be me."

What can
I do?

Let's make
a plan.

Solving a Problem

1. Identify the problem.

2. Gather the facts.

3. Make a plan.

4. Carry out the plan.

"I thought you could help me; that you would know best.
Provide some advice, that would help with my quest."
"Yes," replied Ruru, "I'm sure that I can.
But when solving a problem, you must first have a plan."

"Gather the information, all that you need,
before setting a course, on a path to succeed.
So questions for you Tūī, I do have a few,
before I can give you hints, tips or a clue."

"Where was the place where you last had your feathers?
And what was it like, I mean, how was the weather?"
"On Tāne Mahuta," said Tūī, "I had them there without fail.
There was a westerly wind, it was blowing a gale."

"A-ha," replied Ruru. "I now have a plan.
Return to Tāne Mahuta, and go east young man.
For in an easterly direction, from that giant kauri tree,
your tuft of white feathers, may very well be."

Tāne Mahuta

So Tūī returned to Tāne, to the very same perch,
to begin again, to restart his search.
For the tuft of feathers, that hung under his beak.
That tuft of white feathers, that made him unique.

A chirpy voice soon said, "Hello, who are you?"
It was Pīwakawaka, the fantail, a friend Tūī knew.

"It's me!" exclaimed Tūī. "You know me real well."
"Sorry," cheeped Pīwakawaka. "I just could not tell.
Without your white tuft, you don't ring any bells."

Tūī hung his head down, feeling a little depressed.
"I really don't know, how I'll get out of this mess.
I'm not who I am, it's tough, can't you see?
Without my white tuft, I just can't be me."

"Don't worry," said Pīwakawaka. "I'll help you my friend.
I'm sure all will be well, at least in the end.
I have a real talent, for snapping up things.
If they drift in the wind, they'll be caught on the wing."

As Tūī and his friend, travelled eastwards together,
something floated midair, much like a feather.
It was light, it was white, it gently fluttered by.
"I've got it," cried Pīwakawaka, as he plucked it from the sky.

9

"Darn it!" she said. "It was worth a try.
A nice meal for me, but only a white butterfly."

The sun was going down, as the two journeyed on.
"Tī-e-ke-ke-ke-ke," they heard the saddleback's song.
"Hi, Pīwakawaka," sang Tīeke. "Who's your new mate?
I'd like to make friends. Having friends is so great."

"It's me!" sobbed Tūī. "You know me real well."
"Whoops," chortled Tīeke. "I just could not tell.
Without your white tuft, you don't ring any bells."

Tūī wiped his eyes, feeling down in the dumps.
"I really don't know, how I'll get out of this slump.
I'm not who I am, it's tough, can't you see?
Without my white tuft, I just can't be me."

"Don't worry," said Tīeke. "I'll help you bro.
With me on the job, your problem will go.
I have a real talent, for dealing with sticks.
With my very strong beak, they're gone in a flick."

They hadn't gone far, when Tīeke spotted something white.
Deep in the leaf litter, almost out of sight.
"I'll get it," shrieked Tīeke, as he went straight to work,
sending twigs flying, with a flick or a jerk.

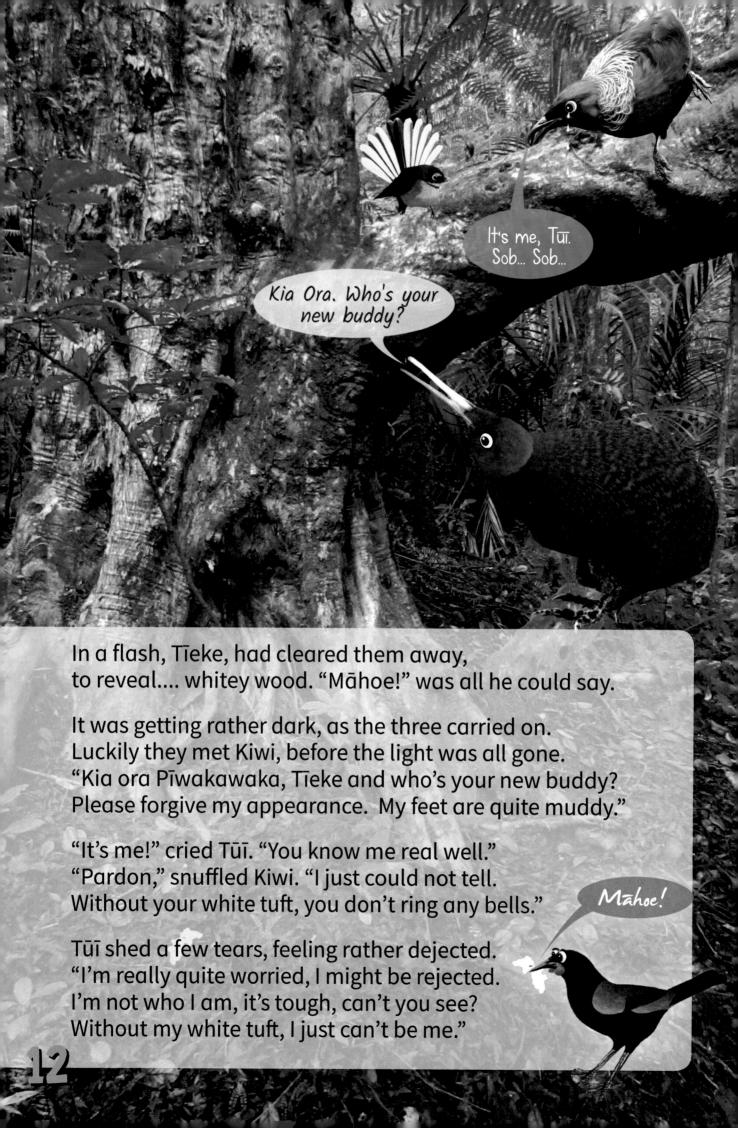

In a flash, Tīeke, had cleared them away,
to reveal.... whitey wood. "Māhoe!" was all he could say.

It was getting rather dark, as the three carried on.
Luckily they met Kiwi, before the light was all gone.
"Kia ora Pīwakawaka, Tīeke and who's your new buddy?
Please forgive my appearance. My feet are quite muddy."

"It's me!" cried Tūī. "You know me real well."
"Pardon," snuffled Kiwi. "I just could not tell.
Without your white tuft, you don't ring any bells."

Tūī shed a few tears, feeling rather dejected.
"I'm really quite worried, I might be rejected.
I'm not who I am, it's tough, can't you see?
Without my white tuft, I just can't be me."

"Don't worry," said Kiwi. "I'll help you, e hoa.
Your troubles will become extinct. Just like the moa.
I have a real talent, for sniffing out stuff.
With nostrils on my bill tip, one whiff is enough."

"I'm picking up a scent," snorted Kiwi, as he left at a jog.
"It's coming from inside, this old rotten log."
Probing and scratching, no effort was spared.
"I have it. I have it," Kiwi declared.

13

Yes, it was soft, it was white, the thing that he found.
Not a feather, but a huhu grub, big, fat and round.

Upside down, on a branch, just hanging around,
Pekapeka, the long-tailed bat, made hardly a sound.
"Greetings Pīwakawaka, Tīeke, Kiwi. Who's your comrade?
His echoes don't tell me, who he is, I'm afraid."

"It's me!" blubbered Tūī. "You know me real well."
"Excuse me," whispered Pekapeka. "I just could not tell.
Without your white tuft, you don't ring any bells."

Tūī by now, was getting rather upset.
He felt almost as low, as low as one gets.
"I'm not who I am, it's tough, can't you see?
Without my white tuft, I just can't be me."

14

"Don't worry," said Pekapeka. "I'll help you my man.
We'll sort this thing out. I'll do what I can.
I have a real talent, for locating things in the dark,
with sound waves I send, that bounce back from their mark."

No sooner had he said that, when Pekapeka exclaimed,
"Thar she blows. I've found it, after just having aimed.
It's fluffy and furry and light in the air.
Maybe it's white? Can you tell if you stare?"

15

Unfortunately again, it just wasn't to be.
For a toetoe flower, was all they could see.

Tūī was nearing the end of his tether,
believing they'd never, find his white feathers.
But just as they were, about to give up the chase,
Kiwi suddenly took off, at a lightning quick pace.

"I just got a whiff, a whiff on the breeze.
Over this way, near the kohekohe trees.
I think they may be, in this cavity nest.
But it's too high for me? Oh, what a pest!"

"Let me do it. I'll fit. I'm good in tight places,"
pleaded Tīeke, as he squeezed into the smallest of spaces.
On closer inspection, he glimpsed something shining.
Woven into the nest, a white tuft, in the lining.

17

"Eureka, it's them. There can be no doubt.
I'll pry them loose. I'll lever them out."
But just as Tīeke, had the problem all sussed,
a matangi, a breeze, blew with a sudden quick gust.

The tuft of white feathers disappeared in a jiffy.
"Fodgity podge!" cried Tūī, his nostrils all sniffy.
Pekapeka let loose, firing off sound waves galore.
Scanning for echoes, to locate them once more.

"Over there by the karaka, they're twirling about."
"My turn," piped up Pīwakawaka, "my turn to help out."
She darted across, she twisted and tumbled.
Then snatched the tuft up, for she never fumbled.

Tūī's face lit up, like pōhutukawa in bloom.
A blaze of happiness, with no hint of gloom.
"Oh thank you, oh thank you, you're all such good friends.
To help me to be, who I am, once again."

Like a lightbulb Tūī's face, suddenly switched off.
One moment so bright, the next dull, like a moth.
"I have my white tuft back, with the plan Ruru hatched.
But the problem is now, how can they be reattached?"

The friends all fell silent, for a moment, a tick.
When Pīwakawaka announced, with a proud tail flick,
"Let's go see Ruru, he'll know what to do.
His wisdom, his knowledge, will surely shine through."

So off the five went, to Ruru's pūruri tree perch,
for an answer so Tūī, wasn't left in the lurch.
After some thinking time, Ruru's solution was heard.
"You all know young Hihi, he's the little stitchbird."

For an instant the five, all looked a little perplexed.
Then it dawned on them all, what they had to do next.
"Hihi's a stitchbird, he can sew Tūī's feathers back on,"
sang the five friends in chorus, in a chorus of song.

That little ray of sunshine!

"Thank you Ruru," squealed Tūī, "for your fine words of wisdom.
You're the cleverest bird, in the whole animal kingdom."
"St-i-t-ch --- St-i-t-ch," came a call, from a kowhai in flower.
"There's Hihi over there, sipping a sweet nectar shower."

23

I hear him.

"Hi Hihi," chortled Tūī. "Please do me a favour?
Would you take a wee break, from the food that you savour?
My tuft of white feathers, broke off in the wind.
Would you sew them back on, here under my chin?"

"Of course, dear Tūī, you must've been doing it tough,
to lose something so special, to lose real Tūī stuff.
Stand still while I grab, my pine needle and thread.
Not made of cotton, but harakeke instead."

Hihi sewed swiftly and deftly, with stitches so fine.
Not one soft white feather, did he stitch out of line.
"Yippy yai yay," screeched Tūī. "I'm Tūī once more.
Thanks heaps Hihi. I'm just like before."

To celebrate the five, partied all day and all night,
with Ruru and Hihi, who they were sure to invite.
Tūī's mates all knew, who he was once again.
And didn't have to say, "Hey, who's your new friend?"

Learn More about the Forest & Friends!

TŪĪ were called the parson's bird by early European settlers because of the small tuft of white feathers on their necks. Tūī have a double voice box which enables them to combine melodic notes with clicks, cackles, creaks and wheezing sounds. Tūī are also great mimickers with the ability to replicate the calls of other birds, phone ring tones, car alarms and even human speech. Māori sometimes kept tūī as pets, with one Māori chief training his tūī to perform a mihi (greeting) when guests arrived. The Māori quickly learned however to keep their tūī at the other end of the village to their kuri (dogs) otherwise the tūī would soon mimic their barking.

Ruru (*morepork*) are New Zealand's only surviving native owl, known for their haunting melancholic call, which is reflected in its name. Ruru are nocturnal, hunting at night for large invertebrates including beetles, weta, moths and spiders. They will also prey on small birds, rats and mice. Ruru can turn their heads through 270 degrees. They fly silently as they have soft fringes on the edge of their wing feathers, catching their prey using their large sharp talons or beaks. By day they roost in the cavities of trees or in thick vegetation. If they are visible during the day, they can get mobbed by other birds and are forced to move.

Pīwakawaka (*fantail*) are small insectivorous birds which have the ability to catch their prey on the wing. They will often follow other birds through the forest, such as families of pōpokotea (whiteheads), catching any flying insects disturbed by the pōpokotea as they scour the branches of trees.

Tīeke (*saddleback*) are a member of the endemic wattle bird family, which also includes the kōkako and the extinct huia. Unlike crocodiles, which have strong muscles for closing their jaws, tīeke have strong muscles for opening their beaks, allowing them to easily flick up sticks in the leaf litter or to pry off bark from a tree when looking for insects. Its Māori name comes from its territorial tī-e-ke-ke-ke-ke call, which can sound like someone trying to start up a car motor. Its English name is derived from the brown plumage on its back which resembles a saddle.

Tīeke traditionally held a strong place in Māori superstitious belief; their cries were viewed as good omens when heard from the right, and bad omens when heard from the left. Its cheeky nature is reflected in the Māori legend that tells how the bird acquired its distinctive chestnut coloured saddle. Fresh from his battle to slow down the sun, a thirsty Māui asked Tīeke to bring him some water. Tīeke pretended not to hear Māui's request. Māui became so angry he seized Tīeke with his hand, which was still hot, leaving a brown scorch mark across its back.

Kiwi are New Zealand's iconic bird but could be referred to as an honorary mammal because of its many mammalian characteristics and habits. It has shaggy hair-like plumage and cat-like whiskers around the face and at the base of the beak. It has powerful muscular legs with heavy marrow-filled bones, whereas most bird skeletons are light and filled with air sacs to enable flight. It has a body temperature of 37-38°C, whereas a bird's body temperature ranges from 39-42°C. It has a highly developed sense of smell with nostrils at the end of its beak, a keen sense of hearing with large visible ear openings and two ovaries instead of one. The chick emerges from an enormous egg as a mini adult, able to feed itself (unusual for birds). It builds a burrow like a badger and it is flightless.

Pekapeka (*long-tailed bat or lesser short-tailed bat*) are New Zealand's only native land mammals. Pekapeka navigate and catch insects at night by bouncing high-frequency sounds off their surroundings. This activity, called 'echolocation', gives them a detailed picture of their environment using sound waves rather than light. Pekapeka can fly at over 60 km per hour and they will often fly further than 50 km in a night to a favourite feeding site. Pekapeka feed on a diet of flying insects; mainly moths, midges, mosquitoes and beetles. They can use a membrane along the full length of their tails to scoop up insects on the wing.

Hihi (*stitchbird*) are one of New Zealand's rarest birds. Although they compete with tūī and korimako for nectar, fruit and insects, they share very few other qualities. DNA evidence shows that they are the sole representative of a bird family found only in New Zealand. Male and female hihi look quite different, with the male displaying a more colourful plumage, including a black head, white ear tufts and a yellow band around the chest. Māori named them hihi, meaning 'ray of sunshine', after this yellow band. Female hihi are greyish brown with white wingbars. Both sexes have small cat-like whiskers around their beaks.

Hihi can be recognised by their upward tilted tail and distinctive call, which sounds a little like two stones being repeatedly struck together. A 19th century ornithologist described the call made by the male hihi as resembling the word 'stitch'. This description led to hihi also being known as the stitchbird. During the breeding season the female builds a complex nest in a tree cavity using 200-600 sticks as a base. This is topped with a nest cup of finer twigs and lined with fern scales, lichen and spider webs. Males will mate with as many females as possible, resulting in a single clutch of eggs potentially having 5 or 6 fathers. Hihi are the only birds known to sometimes mate face to face.

Pūriri are evergreen trees endemic to New Zealand. They are an important source of food for birds, especially in winter, as they can produce pink nectar-producing flowers and berries (red when ripe) all year round. Māori made infusions from boiled pūriri leaves to bathe sprains, relieve backache and treat ulcers and sore throats. The timber is very strong and durable and Māori used it for making garden tools and weapons.

Pūriri trees often have holes in their trunks, created by the caterpillar of the native pūriri moth, which lives for 6-7 years in the tree before pupating into a large green moth. The moth lives for only a couple of days because it hasn't got any mouthparts. That's just enough time to find a mate and lay eggs. The pūriri moth is the largest moth in New Zealand, with a wingspan of up to 16 cm. The caterpillar is also very large, growing up to 100 mm long and 15 mm wide. They were regarded as good eating by the Māori, who poured water down their entrance holes to force them out.

Tāne Mahuta is a giant kauri tree in the Waipoua forest in Northland. It is New Zealand's largest known living kauri tree. It is 51.2 metres high and its girth is 13.77 metres. The main trunk is 17.68 m tall and contains 244.5 cubic meters of wood. Its age is unknown, but it is estimated at between 1250 and 2500 years. Its Māori name means "Lord of the Forest". According to the Māori creation myth, Tāne is the son of Ranginui, the sky father and Papatūānuku, the earth mother. Tāne separates his parents from their marital embrace until his father the sky is high above mother earth. Tāne then sets about clothing his mother with vegetation. The birds and the trees of the forest are regarded as Tāne's children.

Māhoe *(whitey wood)* are small trees identifiable by their light coloured bark. Their trunks and branches are often covered in patches of white lichen, giving them their common name. The wood was too brittle for Māori to use for making paddles, but it was good for starting fires. This was done by rubbing a flat piece of māhoe vigorously with a pointed piece of hard kaikōmako. Female trees produce striking purple berries during the late summer months and on into autumn. This fruit is eaten by tūī, kererū and geckos.

Kohekohe trees have a tropical origin and grow naturally in the warmer parts of New Zealand. They have large green glossy leaves. As is common with other trees found in tropical rainforests, the waxy white sprays of flowers that appear in May/June, sprout directly from the branches or trunk of the tree. This phenomenon is called cauliflory which translates as "stem flowers". Birds eat the red fleshy seed covering once the seed capsules have developed and split.

Karaka trees have glossy green leaves and large fleshy orange fruit with a poisonous kernel. However the kernel was an important source of protein for the Māori who developed a specific process to destroy the toxins. The kernels were cooked or steamed for up to 2 days and then placed in woven baskets (kete) and submerged in running water. Once dried in the sun, they could then be stored until eaten.

Pōhutukawa are New Zealand's Christmas tree as they are covered in bright red flowers during December. It is a hardy coastal plant with its leaves adapted to wind and salt spray. A layer of felt-like hairs on the underside of the leaves helps to reduce moisture loss, thus enabling the pōhutukawa to survive drought conditions. The flowers are an important source of nectar for birds, geckos and insects.

Kōwhai means yellow in Māori, so the Māori named this native tree after its profusion of yellow flowers that appear in spring. It is an important source of food for the nectar-feeding birds like the tūī, korimako (bellbird) and hihi. The Māori used kōwhai for medicinal purposes. The bark of the kōwhai tree was heated in a calabash with hot stones, then made into a poultice for wounds or rubbed onto a sore back. Wai kōwhai (kōwhai juice) was applied to the bite wounds inflicted by seals and the lesions would heal within days.

Harakeke (*flax*) is a plant unique to New Zealand and was an important fibre for Māori, who used it for making kakahu, (clothing), whariki (mats), kono (plates), kete (baskets), taura (ropes), kupenga (nets), aho hī ika (fishing lines), āhere (bird snares) and even rattles for babies. Harakeke also had many Rongoā (medicinal) uses. The sticky sap or gum was applied to boils and wounds and used for toothache. The hard part of the leaf was used to splint broken bones and matted leaves were used as dressings. Root juice was applied to wounds as a disinfectant and bad cuts were sewn up with muka (flax fibre) using a sharpened stick.

References

Department of Conservation - Nature website: http://www.doc.govt.nz/nature

Department of Conservation - Parks & Recreation website:
http://www.doc.govt.nz/parks-and-recreation

Tititiri Matangi Open Sanctuary website:
http://www.tiritirimatangi.org.nz/learn

Rhys Jones. 'Rongoā - medicinal use of plants',
Te Ara - the Encyclopedia of New Zealand website:
http://www.TeAra.govt.nz/en/rongoa-medicinal-use-of-plants

Museum of New Zealand, Te Papa - Māori Medicine (Rongoā) website:
https://www.tepapa.govt.nz/discover-collections/explore/maori/maori-medicine

Published 2017

by Paul Prosée

ISBN: 978-0-473-41870-0

Printed by The Copy Press, Nelson, New Zealand. www.copypress.co.nz

Oh No!!

Poor Tūī has lost his special tuft of white neck feathers!

Tūī is going to need some help from his forest friends, but will they know who he is without his neck tuft?

Follow Tūī as he tries to get his tuft back!

Learning Opportunities

This book provides a variety of potential learning opportunities for teachers and parents, in the following curriculum areas:

English: Rhyming words; contractions; similes and metaphors; interesting action words including communication verbs; different ways of describing feelings of sadness.

Māori: Māori names for endemic and native New Zealand species of fauna and flora. Māori culture, including medicinal uses of native plants.

Science: Characteristics and behaviours of endemic and native New Zealand bird and bat species.

Skills: Problem solving; collaboration.

Values: Using your talents to help your friends; empathy; generosity; persistence; personal identity; self-esteem.

This book is suitable as a shared reading resource for Years 0-3 children and as a guided or independent reading resource for children reading at Early Level 2 and above.

NEW ZEALAND MADE

ISBN: 978-0-473-41870-0

9 780473 418700 >